The doorbell rang, and when Mum opened the door . . .

There was Elvis Presley!

I'm not kidding.

'I was just on my way to a gig,' he said. 'But when I realized who it was, I thought what the hell!' Then he looked at me and said in his Elvis voice, 'Sorry, little lady. I mean *what the heck*.' He was joking of course. At least I hoped he was. If he wasn't, Eddie had a big problem.

'Right!' Mum was practically lost for words. So would you have been.

Eddie's dad was wearing a tight white jumpsuit with tassles on the arms. It split open above his stomach to show off his hairy chest. Vomit city!

ALAN FRASER

13 PAIRS OF BLUE SUEDE SHOES

Illustrated by NIGEL BAINES

CORGI YEARLING BOOKS

THIRTEEN PAIRS OF BLUE SUEDE SHOES
A CORGI YEARLING BOOK : 0 440 86538 7

Published in Great Britain by Corgi Yearling Books,
an imprint of Random House Children's Books

This edition published 2003

Copyright © 2003 by Alan Fraser
Illustrations copyright © 2003 by Nigel Baines

The right of Alan Fraser to be identified as the author of this work has been
asserted in accordance with the Copyright, Designs and Patents Act 1988

Papers used by Random House Children's Books are natural, recyclable
products made from wood grown in sustainable forests. The manufacturing
processes conform to the environmental regulations of the country
of origin.

Set in 15/19pt Bembo Schoolbook

Corgi Yearling Books are published by Random House Children's Books,
61–63 Uxbridge Road, London W5 5SA,
a division of The Random House Group Ltd,
in Australia by Random House Australia (Pty) Ltd,
20 Alfred Street, Milsons Point, Sydney, NSW 2061, Australia,
in New Zealand by Random House New Zealand Ltd,
18 Poland Road, Glenfield, Auckland 10, New Zealand
and in South Africa by Random House (Pty) Ltd,
Endulini, 5a Jubilee Road, Parktown 2193, South Africa

THE RANDOM HOUSE GROUP Limited Reg. No. 954009
www.kidsatrandomhouse.co.uk

A CIP catalogue record for this book is available from the British Library.

Printed and bound in Great Britain by
Cox & Wyman Ltd., Reading, Berkshire.

For Trish, Katie and Nic.
With a very special thank you
to Lucy Hadley

1

ON THE WALL

Jack's mum was in *Grange Hill*.

Karen's dad played football for Notts Forest.

Julie's uncle's got a Rolls Royce. So she says.

Bipin's dad sailed round the world.

Sally's mum speaks five languages. And one of them's Russian!

My dad sings in a male voice choir.

Guess who got the big laugh?

I thought I might kill Malcolm Middleton.

me

I'm Sam, by the way. And that's
Sam-short-for-Samantha.

We were sitting round at lunch-break, on
our usual bit of wall, talking about being
famous and stuff. Well, Jack couldn't help
himself, could he?

'My mum was in *Grange Hill*.'

Like we hadn't heard it a million times
already! Usually we gave him our yes-we-
think-you-may-have-mentioned-that look
and that's the end of it. But this time Eddie
was with us. And Eddie was new to the
wall. He looked to me like he'd just
beamed down from Planet Zog!

'Really!' he said, all impressed.

So that's when it started – all the bragging about whose dad did this or whose mum did that. It wasn't my idea, believe me. And no way would I bang on about my dad's choir. I'm not a complete dillywag. I mean, I do have some brain cells. It was Malcolm Moron who told everyone. And he didn't say 'Sam's dad's a really good singer'. He said, 'Sam's dad sings in a stupid Welsh choir and he isn't even Welsh!'

I decided I would kill Malcolm Middleton.

So everyone had a good laugh. Apart from Sally – she's my best friend – and Eddie. For some reason he just sat there dead quiet. But they were the only two. All the others went laughing mad. Especially Malcolm Moron. I tried to act cool like I didn't care, because if I hadn't I might've started crying. And don't get me wrong,

9

I'm not usually picked on. Usually, I get by OK.

Maybe I could arrange a swimming party and hire a shark. 'Come on, Malcolm! First one to the other side.'

HOME TO MY HOUSE

Our school's not that big – nothing in Wottney is. And usually I quite like school. I don't live for it like some sad spotty swotty, I just quite like it. But I was glad to get away that afternoon. In fact I went out the gates double quick. Sally was with me. We usually walk home together. It's not far – nowhere in Wottney is.

Sally could tell Moron had got to me.

'Look, Sam, it's only Malcolm Middleton. You know what he's like.'

'Yeah, I know what he's like all right.

He's a double-decker duffbucket who had everyone laughing at my dad.'

'Not everyone. I wasn't laughing.'

– 'I should hope not!'

'Nor was Eddie.' Sally had noticed that too.

'You're right,' I said, all determined. 'It is only Malcolm Moron, isn't it! And why should I let that drongo wind me up?'

Sally smiled. 'Is that your name for him – Malcolm Moron?'

'Just one of them. I've quite a few stored up and I feel loads more coming on!'

'Like . . .'

'Well . . . like Malcolm Mouse-Droppings, or Malcolm Muckspreader or Malcolm Missing-Link, or Malcolm Mind-the-Gap, or Malcolm Mustypants, or Malcolm Mystery-Tour, or Malcolm Muppet-Brain, or Malcolm Mooningbum.'

Sally laughed.

And so did I.

'So tell me about Eddie,' I said. It was Sally who'd brought him to the wall. Sally's good like that.

'Not much to tell,' she said. 'He's just moved to the new houses behind the rec. They've come from Stevenage, wherever that is. His dad's a plasterer.'

'Right.'

'Or is it a plumber?'

I had no idea. And anyway, by then, we'd got to my house. I told you it wasn't far.

'You coming in?' I asked.

'Best not.' Sally held up her schoolbag. 'Fings to do.'

'Teacher's pet!'

'Slacker!'

Our house isn't that special. We are talking Wottney, remember. But at least it's

built from proper red bricks and has a nice front door with a stained-glass panel.

'Anyone in?' I called, pushing it open.

There wasn't. Mum works part-time at the vet's and Dad hardly ever leaves his office 'til six. And don't ask me what he does there because it's one of those jobs that can't be explained. And if you ask him to try you feel your brain melting.

So I was used to finding the house empty. And the first thing I always do is go to the kitchen for a drink.

Well – can you believe it? – I started thinking about Malcolm Muckspreader and the wall.

Again!

I should have got a grip. I should have turned on the radio. I should have put it out my head. Because – for half a milli-second – I did something I'd never done before. I wished my dad didn't sing at all.

It still makes me shiver.

I mean, my dad not singing wouldn't be my dad.

When I was six or seven, I went to all his concerts. And I wasn't dragged along screaming and kicking. And I didn't sit at the back sulking. I actually enjoyed it. I really did. I bet I can still sing the songs.

Just never, never, *never* ask me to prove it!

And he is a good singer. And he really loves to sing. But I never go to hear him now. Not that I'm Princess Superior or anything. It's the awful choir thing I can't stand — with their gross purple blazers and their puke-awful ties. It's just so un-believably *naff*. And all that Welsh stuff when only half of them are. My dad is a bit because Grandad came from the Rhondda. So Muckspreader was wrong about that. But Dad doesn't sound Welsh at all. Not like Mr Williams — he's so Welsh he comes from a place you can't pronounce, and if you try to, you spray half the room with spit!

Mr Williams is the choirmaster.

I LEARN EDDIE'S SECRET

On Saturday we usually have breakfast together – me, Mum and Dad. It's not my idea believe me. And nor is it Mum's. It's Dad who thinks it's dead significant. He even lays out the breakfast things. Round of applause! 'We don't have to rush about today,' he says, 'so let's be a proper family and talk around the table.' Then we all sit in silence and listen to the radio. Which is OK with Mum – she's in the Land of Zombie 'til her third cup of tea. And it's OK with me – I don't care either way. And, actually, it's OK with Dad too. Because Dad loves Saturday radio – in fact, if you try to talk to him he says, 'Hang on, I'm just listening to this!'

It's nice being a proper family.

The radio show that morning was all about adrenaline junkies. You know the sort of people – surfers, bungee jumpers, skydivers, snowboarders and stuff. After two minutes Mum lifted her head, mumbled 'Nutters' then reached for the teapot. Dad looked across like he was thinking 'I'm not so sure about that.' Me, I thought they were all brilliant. 'It's the rush, man. It's the rush!' one surfer was saying. I bet he had a bandanna.

I could have done with a bit of rush myself.

'I think I'll go into town,' I said. You'd think I'd know better — shopping in Wottney's not exactly a white-knuckle-ride.

'OK Smidge,' said Dad. Mum sort of grunted.

I was in WH Smiths when it happened.

I was wandering about the shop — checking out the hundreds of CDs I can't afford — and he sort of appeared. Like he really had beamed down.

'Hello, Sam,' he said.

It was Eddie.

'Oh, hi,' I said.

Well I could hardly ignore him, could I? And, actually, I didn't want to. So we kind of talked about this 'n that — I won't tell you what, you wouldn't be impressed. We just sort of rambled for a bit — until we got to one of those embarrassing silences. And then, for some reason, don't ask me why, I heard myself saying, 'Thanks for not laughing, you know, about my dad's choir, yesterday, on the wall.'

'That's all right,' he said. 'My dad's a singer too.'

'Is he?'

'Fraid so.'

'He's not Welsh, is he?'

'No,' said Eddie, as if I hadn't made a hilarious joke. 'He's not Welsh. I only wish he was.'

'Why's that?'

'He's . . .'

'Yes?'

'He's . . .'

'What?'

'He's . . .'

'Listen Eddie, we could make a career out of this. But I was planning something slightly more interesting. If you don't want to tell . . .'

'He's . . .'

'Yes.'

'He's . . .'

'Eddie!'

'He's an Elvis impersonator.'

An Elvis impersonator.

AN ELVIS IMPERSONATOR!

How sad was that!

In case you don't know, I'll spell it out –
Eddie's dad dresses up in stupid clothes and
pretends to be a fat rock-and-roll singer
who died a squillion years ago.

I'm not kidding!

And what makes it all so massively tragic is Elvis was young once – when dinosaurs ruled the Earth – and actually quite cool. I happen to know that because I saw one of his films when I had the flu. But don't think I'm some Elvis anorak, because I'm not.

If I was, I'd have to pretend he didn't get old and fat and corny. Which he most definitely did! And for some stupid reason, *that's* the Elvis they always copy.

When Eddie told me, I didn't know what to say. I think I said, 'Oh, really.' But I didn't laugh. I'm not Malcolm Mindless.

And when he looked at me, I could tell – I was Eddie's new friend. How did that happen?

Mum was messing in the garden when I got back.

'I've got something to tell you,' I said.

I had to tell somebody didn't I? And with mums it goes with the job.

'OK,' she said. 'Let's get some tea.'

When I'd finished telling her, Mum said, 'You know what it is, Sam – you've become Eddie's confidante.' That was the word she used – *confidante*. It meant he'd trusted me with a secret. Wow! I thought.

'Why not ask him round next Saturday?' said Mum. 'It's the Wales–England game.'

'I dunno,' I said.

'Well, you don't have to.'

'Maybe I will.'

'Good.'

And that was that. Mum went back to her garden and I sat there taking it in – being Eddie's confidante and everything. And, actually, it felt all right. I mean I wouldn't be skipping down the road going tra-la-la, or grinning at myself in mirrors. But Eddie was OK. It wasn't fair what I said about Planet Zog. He'd never be Mr Popularity. But so what?

4

EDDIE LEARNS MY SECRET

First thing on a Monday — first thing! — Pop Fussell had us just where he wants us, which means sitting in his classroom for fifty minutes of mathematical torture. How cruel is that! It's bad enough wondering where the weekend went.

And to think I used to like Maths — when I was seven or eight. I even won a competition! Girl genius. But Pop Fussell sorted all that in two and a half lessons. Professor Turn-off. You'd think he'd try a bit harder, wouldn't you? I mean, imagine spending your whole life looking at hundreds of kids who want to be somewhere else. Trouble is, I don't think he even knows. I knew he'd got me wrong. He even told my dad I had the *makings of a fine mathematician*. Me! After what it's done for him. No thanks.

And anyway, I had a different plan. But I didn't spread it about and only a few people knew. Mum and Dad knew, and Miss Dapple, and Sally of course, and probably her mum. But that was it.

Until that lunch-time.

Me, Sally and Eddie were sitting round our sarnies, recovering from Pop Fussell's percentages and fractions. Eddie wanted to know about Sally's mum. Because Sally's mum's a teacher at our school.

But it was no big deal. Sally was really cool about it.

'She does French and Spanish,' she explained.

I was about to add we might have her next year. Then *he* interrupted.

'Hey, you three!'

I recognized the voice straight off and so did Sally – I could tell from the look on her face. Malcolm Mindless was marching across the room.

'There's no chips!' he said.

Like, why was he telling us?

'No chips! Not one tray!' he moaned.

Did he think we were best buddies or something?

'There's rice and pasta.'

He might easily have said *rotting fish and maggots.*

'But no chips?' Sally prompted.

'None! No chips at all! And the dinner ladies said there won't be, except on Fridays!'

Mindless loved his chips. Everybody said so. And you could tell from his size he really put them away. It was chips that made his school dinners worth having. So not having chips must have put him into some type of shock. Good! I expect that's why he told us. He needed to tell someone, and we were it.

He even sat down.

'No chips!' he repeated – in case we hadn't grasped his point.

This next bit didn't happen. I'm making it up.

'So, Eddie. What's your dad do?' asked Malcolm.

'He's a plumber.'

'Mine's an architect.'

'Wow! That's really cool! I wish my dad was an architect. And not just a boring old plumber. He's not interesting at all. Not like your dad. Gosh he must be dead clever and earn loads of money. Wow!'

Malcolm would have loved that.

What really happened was this.

'What's your dad do?'

'He's a plumber.'

'Mine's an architect.'

'Oh.'

Nothing. End of conversation. Hooray.

So Mugwump got up — muttered something about chips — and left. Double hooray with extra chocolate!

And that's when I told Eddie — while the word was drifting about.

'I'm going to be an architect.'

Sally stopped chewing her sandwich.

'Really?' said Eddie. 'You mean like Malcolm's dad?'

'What, Mr Sunday Golf! No way! His idea of architecture is building nasty little boxes and calling them *detached family homes*. That's not architecture.'

'Isn't it?' said Eddie.

'No,' I said. 'That's rubbish.'

'Sam wants to be a proper architect,' said Sally.

'Like Gaudi,' I said.

'Who's Gaudi?' asked Eddie.

Sally bit off a mouthful and gave me a look. She probably thought I was about to go on a bit. I can do that sometimes. I'm not perfect.

'Why don't you come to my house on Saturday,' I said instead. 'I can show you some pictures. Plus it's the Wales–England game. Sally'll come, won't you, Sal?'

'Course,' she said.

'What's the Wales–England game?' asked Eddie.

Eddie had a lot to learn.

WHY I WANT TO BE AN ARCHITECT

I got home at three twenty-two and had a drink. Then I went upstairs to look at my Gaudi books. I never get bored with them.

In case you don't know, Antoni Gaudi is Spain's best-loved architect. For most of his life he lived in Barcelona, which is why Barcelona is full of his buildings, and why I'm desperate to get there.

I think I'd better explain.

It's quite a long story.

At Christmas my mum brings out the

table-mats. Never any other time. Just Christmas. Don't ask me why.

Anyway, on the mats are these brilliant paintings. I've always liked them — especially the rich, swirling colours. But I didn't know who'd painted them. Not until two years ago when I caught the chicken-pox. Because lying on the sofa — bravely NOT scratching — I saw this film called *Lust for Life*. And I realized — it was about the man who did the paintings on the mats. It was about Vincent Van Gogh. And did his life suck! The really sad thing was he never knew how great he was. In his whole lifetime, he never sold a single paint-ing. Not properly.

And now they put him on table-mats.

Well, when my spots disappeared, when I could scratch but didn't want to, when

Dad said, 'Would you like a bit of a treat, Smidge?', I said, 'Can we go to an Art Gallery?'

The film had got me curious.

So we did.

It was totally brilliant – enormous rooms full of colour.

And that's when I decided I wanted to be a painter. I mean, I'd always liked painting at school and on the kitchen table, but now I wanted to do it for a job.

And for ages that's *all* I wanted. Trouble is – I can admit it now – I wasn't that good. I had loads of ideas but they all came out wrong. I must've gone through a million sheets of paper – just trying and trying and trying. And the really hard thing was loads of my friends – who didn't really care – were better than I was.

I remember one day we had to paint this tatty stuffed owl thing. Sally's painting was really good but my effort looked like a great lump of porridge.

'It's rubbish,' I said. 'I'm rubbish.'

'No you're not,' said Sally.

'Well, I wish my owl looked like yours,' I said.

'And I wish I was good at Maths.'

I know she was trying to make me feel better, but it didn't help. I just wished I could swap with her. My Maths for her painting.

And then – in fact, the week after – I went ice-skating and sprained my ankle. Don't ask me how. Let's just say, one day Julie will pay!

So I was lying on the sofa watching telly, tapping the remote like you do, when suddenly I saw this amazing building. I couldn't believe it. It was so totally brilliant my ankle stopped throbbing! And *then* they showed another building – just as amazing – and then *another*! So that was it. That's how I discovered Gaudi. On a travel programme about Barcelona.

Well, as soon as I stopped hobbling about, I went to the library and found a Gaudi book. I was so excited I ended up reading it in the street. Now I've got

pictures of his buildings stuck around my bedroom. And I've got two books about him on my shelf. I suppose I'm a bit of a Gaudi anorak. Sad or what? I don't care.

His stuff was wild.

I mean, think of a building. Any size. Give it turrets and towers and balconies – as many as you like. Make it fantastic – really fantastic. Now twist the shape about. Cover it in fabulous mosaics. Or amazing animal figures. Or weird swirling metalwork. Let your imagination go crazy.

You aren't even close!

He's the reason I want to be an architect.

Because what he did was like painting with buildings. Except with buildings you don't have to be *that* brilliant with a paintbrush. You just need to get your ideas across. Which I bet I can. I'm not that duffo.

And the best thing is, buildings are for everyone. I mean, everyone in Barcelona loves Gaudi – not just the snobby rich people, but everyone. That's the thing about buildings. They're not like a Van Gogh painting. You don't have to be dead fifty years before people get the point. Buildings are in your face.

As soon as I got the chance, I was going to Barcelona.

THE DAY OF THE RUGBY MATCH

We were up in my bedroom. I was showing Eddie my Gaudi posters. Sally'd seen them loads already.

'They're like Disney,' said Eddie.

He was trying to be complimentary, I suppose.

'No, Eddie,' I said. 'They're NOT like Disney.'

'Sorry.'

'They are a bit,' said Sally.

I gave her my look.

'But Gaudi's a million times better,' she

said. 'I mean, anyone can see that, can't they?' Sally looked across at Eddie.

'Oh yes,' said Eddie. 'Anyone can see that.' He couldn't of course, but it was a nice try.

'Well, OK,' I said, 'they are a *bit* like Disney.'

Downstairs we could hear the party. The singing had started, which meant the game had finished. Don't ask me who'd won – I can never see the point of rugby. So I couldn't care less. Not like my dad. Mr Rugby-is-my-Life.

When I had the mumps I saw this ancient film called *The Night of the Werewolves*. What happens is this – quite normal people with barbecues and everything turn into blood-crazy wolf-creatures every time there's a full moon. Well, it's the same with my dad when Wales play England at rugby. He doesn't actually tear out your throat, but if you were an English rugby-player, he wouldn't mind standing on your head. And he starts using all these funny Welsh words. He even sounds a bit like Mr Williams.

'But Dad!' I tell him. 'Grandma comes from Tunbridge Wells and you were born in Tooting.'

'Today I'm Welsh, *cariad*. Today I'm Welsh.'

Well, this was one of those days. So half the choir was in the living room – all red in the face, shouty loud, and full of beer. Soon the wives and girlfriends would come round for a bit of a party. They usually did. And Guy – he's Mervyn's boyfriend.

And I'm glad they have their parties. If they didn't I wouldn't get to hear them sing like they do.

Before a proper concert, Mr Williams always says, 'Dignity, boys. That's what I want. Dignity.' *Dignity* means dressing like you tear tickets at the cinema, standing like you're frozen solid from the neck down, and looking like your close relations must be some type of goldfish. I'm not joking.

But after a rugby match, they sway about, close their eyes, and just sing. It sounds much better. Like they're really enjoying it. That's what I think anyway. And this Saturday they were *really* going for it.

'Come on,' I said to Eddie and Sally. 'Let's go down. It's quite fun.'

'My dad does that song,' said Eddie, halfway down the stairs. They were singing *John Brown's Body*.

'You're kidding,' I said. It didn't sound very rock and roll to me.

'Is your dad a singer?' Sally asked.

Ah! Sally was about to become a confidante.

NEWS OF THE SCHOOL EXCHANGE

I heard the news on Tuesday morning.

Year Ten was going to Barcelona.

Year pigging Ten! We go to Cadbury World. They go to Barcelona. How cruel was that?

It was Sally who told me. She was waiting by the wall when I got to school. I could tell she had some big news.

'Guess what?' she said.

'What?'

'My mum's going to Barcelona.'

'You're joking!' Sally knew I couldn't wait to go there.

'I'm not. There's going to be a school exchange – some time this summer. Year Ten are going and she's going with them.'

'To Barcelona!'

'Yes.'

'But listen, Sam – my mum says that if it's successful, they'll do it again, probably. So one day, well, *we* might get the chance!'

'You reckon?'

'Why not?'

'Right,' I said taking it in.

And I tried to imagine it happening. I really did. But somehow I just couldn't see it. I mean, work it out – if there was going to be an exchange, then a load of Spanish kids from Barcelona were coming to Wottney. And lucky them, I didn't think. Barcelona had Gaudi. And sunshine. And the Mediterranean. And football. And cafés and shops. And masses more I didn't even know about. Yet.

Wottney had a Co-op with an escalator.

They could spend all day going up and down.

I just hoped I was wrong. I really did. I hoped they'd have a brilliant time. I hoped they'd go home buzzing. I hoped a holiday in Wottney would become the star prize on Spanish quiz shows.

Because what I really wanted — more than a ton of free chocolate — were lots of happy Spanish kids telling their friends they must come to Wottney. Year after year after year.

Then Sally would be right.

Then we might get our chance.

WE GET A VISIT FROM THE PLUMBER

One nice thing about our house is the kitchen table. It's really old and oak and used to belong to my gran. So it's seen a lot of teapot action. Dad says she drank more tea than Mum does, which is hard to believe, I can tell you.

I really love our table.

And it's quite big – so when I'm drawing and painting I can easily spread out. And sometimes you *have* to be messy, don't you?

What I specially like is doing architecture competitions. They're not for real of course – I mean, I'm not Princess Loonypants. But they are dead fun. Dad thought it all up one Saturday breakfast.

'Did you hear that?' he said. Meaning the bit on the radio.

Mum grunted. Meaning 'no'.

But I'd heard it. Meaning all these big-time architects wanted to build some Opera House so they'd sent in their ideas to be judged by a panel – like it was a competition.

'You should do that, Smidge,' Dad said.

'What d'you mean?' I asked. He couldn't mean me entering – *Schoolgirl Genius Builds Amazing Opera House!*

'Well,' he said, 'when there's a big competition, you know, like with this Opera House, you could design something you'd like to see. You could imagine you were one of the architects. It would be interesting and fun. And good practice – you know how architects have to work to a brief.'

I knew that. Meaning an Opera House had to be an Opera House and not a bowling alley.

So that's how it started. And now, when Dad spots a competition or something like it, he lets me know and I go to work! Usually he tries to get a photograph of where the building will be, because that helps a lot. I mean, sometimes buildings should say look-at-me-look-at-me-look-at-me, and sometimes they should fit in a bit. Miss Dapple taught me that. She's my Art teacher. And *yes*, that is her real name.

And Dad was right – it is good practice. So far I've designed an Opera House, the Scottish Parliament, a national Sports Stadium and an Art Gallery. Plus I've redesigned Trafalgar Square. No job's too big! I think my stadium's the best thing I've done. I went a bit Gaudi on that one – I couldn't help it. And it's miles better than what they really came up with – which looked like someone had dropped a big jelly.

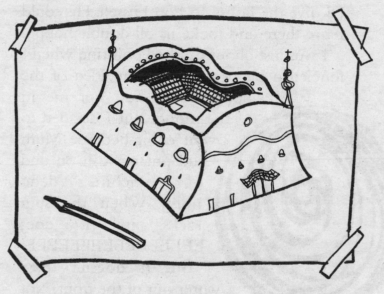

Anyway, this Sunday, I had the kitchen to myself. I was just messing about – painting a desert island beach-house. I'd imagined it all made from wood, with the planking painted pink and green and white. It had a nice sea-sidey pier going into the water and a roof terrace with a telescope and a sunshade in the shape of a sail. I thought it looked brilliant and I still do. But I wouldn't want to live there – I mean, if it was real. A desert island might get a bit boring, mightn't it? So I imagined I'd give the house to Pop Fussell. He could retire there and make us all double happy.

I was just about finished painting when I fancied a bit of reggae – the idea of the beach-house had got me in the mood. But I decided to wait a bit because Mum had put a wash on and our machine's dead noisy. When the spin kicks in, it goes EEEEEEEEEEEEEEEE! But it doesn't spew water out of the front. Not normally anyway!

'Mum!' I called. Dad was out at choir praccy. 'There's water everywhere.'

Mum ran through and clocked the little pool on the floor. It wasn't actually every-where. Sometimes I exaggerate.

'Right, Sam,' she said. 'We just need to be logical.'

So we were. It wasn't that hard — we rang Eddie's dad.

'He's coming round,' she said hanging up the phone.

Well, two minutes later the doorbell rang, and when mum opened the door . . .

There was Elvis Presley!

I'm not kidding.

'I was just on my way to a gig,' he said. 'But when I realized who it was, I thought what the hell!' Then he looked at me and said in his Elvis voice, 'Sorry, little lady. I mean *what the heck.*' He was joking, of course. At least I hoped he was.

If he wasn't, Eddie had a big problem.

'Right!' Mum was practically lost for words. So would you have been.

Eddie's dad was wearing a tight white jumpsuit with tassles on the arms. It split open above his stomach to show off his hairy chest. Vomit city! The enormous collar was covered in joking jewels. So was the big fat belt. And the trousers were flared out over silver boots with clumpy heels. But the best bit – better than his gross sunglasses – was his hair. He had this huge black wig on, all combed back, and big stick-on sideburns.

Get the picture?

'So where's the problem then?' he asked, putting down the bag he was carrying.

'Um . . . the . . . er . . .' Mum pointed at the puddle. I thought, *Mother, close your mouth!*

'Okeydoke,' he said unzipping his bag. Out came a few tools, and a set of overalls, which he stepped into. Then he got fixing. It was the seal apparently. It only took ten minutes to put it right.

'So,' he said bagging up his overalls. 'I

expect it was a bit of a shock seeing me dressed up like this.'

'Oh no,' said Mum.

I gave her a look. *You don't really expect him to believe that, surely!*

'Well, actually,' said Mum, getting real, 'it was a bit.'

'I do it when I'm asked,' he explained. 'Usually, it's for charity. At least that's how it started out. It was just a bit of a laugh at first, but it turns out people really like it, and I don't like to say no. But it is just a laugh. And actually, between you and me, it's not really my thing – Elvis Presley. He's OK, but actually, I'm more of a Willie Nelson man.'

'Right,' said Mum with a smile.

'Okeydoke,' said Elvis.

After he'd driven off to meet his fans, I looked at Mum and she looked at me.

'Actually,' I said, 'he's more of a Willie Nelson man, you know.'

And we burst out laughing.

Who is Willie Nelson anyway?

I GET SOME MORE NEWS

'Here comes Sally,' said Eddie, looking down the corridor.

'Hey!' she called, running up to us. She looked like she'd won the Lottery or something, and seemed a bit out of breath. But she took a quick gulp and said it straight out. 'I'm going on the Barcelona trip.'

'What!'

'I'm going to Barcelona.'

'Brilliant!' said Eddie.

'How?' I said. I'd gone cold all over.

'There's these spaces on the coach and

because it's in the holidays and because my mum's going, well, I can too. It's a sort of special arrangement. What d'you think?'

'It's brilliant,' Eddie repeated, all enthusiastic.

'Yes,' I agreed. 'Brilliant.' I tried hard to sound as pleased as I could. It wasn't easy, because a great pot of jealousy had been dumped on my head and was dripping down my back. That's how it felt. And Sally was my best friend.

'But that's not all,' she said.

'What?'

Sally studied her nails and smiled a little smile. Princess Suspense or what!

'I can take a friend.'

She could take a friend.

Sally could take a friend!

Everyone must have heard. They probably thought I was dying or something. I was definitely screaming.

SAVING UP FOR BARCELONA

Mum said, 'Of course you can go!'

Dad said, 'That's great, Smidge!'

I knew they'd be pleased.

Now I needed some money.

My parents were fantastic about how much Barcelona would cost – which was a lot – but even so, there were things I wanted to buy myself. I mean I had to get some new clothes, didn't I? I wanted some nice cut-offs, and two or three T-shirts, and a new pair of trainers. And I really wanted a camera. Just a cheap one.

Luckily I had a bit of time to organize my savings campaign. And my birthday was coming up – so that would help. I just hoped this year Auntie Vi would dish up the dosh.

'I always think a present is so much more thoughtful,' she says.

Wrong, Auntie Vi. Wrong, wrong, wrong! Not when it's a 'Make your own Jewellery Set'.

I'd have to drop a couple of hints.

Because I wanted to stuff my ancient piggy-bank with notes and coins. And it felt a bit empty, when I picked it up.

I was giving it a hopeful rattle, when Sally came round. She had some news I needed to hear.

'My mum says some of the Year Tens have dropped out.'

'Are they stupid or something?' I said. How could they not want to go to Barcelona?

'The trouble is,' said Sally, 'it makes it more expensive for everyone else. My mum says there's even talk about cancelling.'

My hands went all limp.

It took ages to pick up the pieces.

ENTER THE SCHOOL ASSOCIATION

'Hello, Sam.'

Sally's mum stopped me outside the school library.

'Hello, Mrs Jenkins,' I said in my speaking-to-teachers voice.

'Sally's told you about the problems with the school exchange.'

'Yes. Last night.'

'Well you're not to worry, Sam. I know what Barcelona means to you and I think it's going to be all right.' She must have seen the relief in my face. 'The School Association is going to give us some money. They'll have to do a bit of fund-raising, of course. But that's nothing new.'

'No,' I said.

'So,' she said.

'*Viva España?*' I suggested.

'*Muy bueno*, Sam. *Muy bueno.*'

Sally's mum's OK.

Our School Association are a load of parents who get together to organize stuff that nobody wants. Nobody with a brain. One of their favourite disasters is called a Seventies Night. The idea is they all dance about to the music that was popular when they were our age. This means the stuff they actually liked before they got too old to keep up. And some of it really sucks. Take my word for it – you don't want to check it out. I mean Mr Worthington – Professor Elbow Patches – is a *big* Seventies fan and that says it all. He once told us 'these songs have stood the test of time'. Yeah, right! This means they were rubbish in the Seventies and they're still rubbish thirty years later.

Sally says her mum hates it when the School Association have fund-raisers. She feels they expect her to go along – because she's a teacher and everything. So she'll definitely have to go to anything they do for the Barcelona trip. Maybe they'd come up with something brilliantly original – like an Eighties Night.

You never know.

MISS DAPPLE'S ART CLASS

Friday is double Art, so it's my favourite.
Miss Dapple is a brilliant teacher. She
dresses a bit eccentric — big dangly
earrings, flowing skirts in dusky colours
and rings on every finger. Pop Fussell
doesn't approve at all. He says teachers
should be an example to their pupils.
Like him, I suppose, ha ha! He gave her
this big lecture in the staffroom apparently. Miss Dapple told me about it
because she knew I'd laugh. And because
she trusts me! We're kindred spirits —

that's what she says. It's why I told her about wanting to be an architect and how much I love Gaudi. She even lent me her own books about him. She's my favourite. She's not like other teachers. Even Sally's mum.

'Right, class,' she said that morning, 'some of you may know about the Year Ten exchange to Barcelona.'

Can you believe it? Some of them didn't know!

'Well,' said Miss Dapple once she'd got the dillywags tuned in. 'The School Association is organizing a cabaret to help pay for the trip.'

A cabaret! So that was what they were doing. I bet it was the talk of the staffroom. And I bet they were all groaning at the thought.

'It might be music or dancing or comedy. We don't know just yet. But a cabaret is an entertainment where the audience sits at tables. And *our* class is to design posters to advertise the cabaret.'

Brilliant! I liked that idea.

'Will it be a competition, Miss?'

'No, Julie. But the posters will need to be a certain standard.'

'Can I design my poster at home?'

'Yes, Malcolm, if you want to. But that doesn't mean you can sit around in class doing nothing.'

I wanted to suggest he could sit in the pottery kiln.

'Anyway,' said Miss Dapple. 'To give you some ideas, I want to show you these.' She opened up one of the enormous books from our Art library. It was full of famous posters and stuff. I liked the film posters best – especially the one for *King Kong*. 'But I want you to be original,' she said. 'Try not to copy anything too closely. Even if you really like it. Use the idea to come up with something fresh.'

I knew straight away what I would do — a picture of The Sacred Family, which is a huge church in Barcelona.  The Spanish call it *La Sagrada Familia* and it's totally amazing. Probably, it's the most amazing church anywhere. You can guess who designed it, can't you?

It was a brilliant Art lesson. Even Mugwump was interested. After class he said, 'I'm going to use my dad's studio for my poster. He's got a digital scanner, a laser printer and everything.'

Well, he would have, wouldn't he? Big deal. It made me want to do my poster all free-hand. Then I'd be the opposite. And better. Miss Dapple said it wasn't a competition, but it was now.

NEWS
ABOUT THE
CABARET

It rained all weekend. But I didn't really care. For one thing there was my poster to design. And by Sunday night I had my ideas roughed out.

Dad came in from choir praccy.

'That looks good, Smidge.'

'Thanks,' I said. 'I just need to know the date and I can do it properly.'

'March the 14th.'

'What?'

'It's going to be on March the 14th.'

'How did you know that?'

'I know because I'm in the show.'

'What!'

'Or rather,' he said, '*we're* in the show. The choir's been asked to sing. Karen's mum's the producer apparently. She phoned Mr Williams last night.'

If you'd had a camera and snapped my expression, I'll bet you'd have carried the photo in your pocket. Then, if anyone asked what *gobsmacked* looked like, you could have showed them.

Somehow, I moved my mouth about until some words fell out. 'You are joking, aren't you?'

I knew he wasn't.

'No. We've got a thirty-minute spot.'

14
ON THE WALL
AGAIN

I don't know who chose our bit of wall. It wasn't me. But you have to sit somewhere, don't you? Pop Fussell thinks it's absurd to sit on a wall. But then he would. *Absurd* is one of his favourite words. He says we should stay in our classrooms or sit on the grass.

Me – I like it on our bit of wall. Especially when it's everybody having a good laugh, or just a few of you having a proper conversation.

That's how it was on Monday – just a few of us.

'I suppose my dad's choir will be all right,' I said.

'Of course they will,' said Karen. She knew that was the right answer. 'That's why my mum asked them.'

'Not a huge joke then?' I looked straight into her face.

'Karen doesn't think that,' said Sally.

'Of course I don't. They'll be the stars of the show! At least they can sing. And the other stuff sounds so lame. Robbie Jones' mum's going to do a comic monologue.'

'A what?'

Karen did a deep snobby voice. 'A comic monologue.'

Sally and Karen giggled at that, but I only managed a bit of a smile.

'Anyway,' said Sally, 'it's not like it's the Christmas disco, it's the School Association. We don't have to be there, do we?'

Sally was right.

'And it's all for Barcelona, isn't it? I wish *I* was going to Barcelona, like you two bees.'

Karen was right.

'And I'm sorry I laughed about your

dad's choir,' she said. 'It was stupid of me. But you know how Malcolm gets everyone going.'

'That's all right,' I said. Karen was forgiven.

We even spent five minutes pulling Muckspreader apart. The way Karen and Sally talked, I almost felt sorry for him. Sally said he was sad and I should ignore him. But then, he hadn't laughed at her dad, had he? And it was hard to ignore someone who shoved things in your face.

Like he did just then.

'Hello, you lot,' he said standing right in front of us. 'What d'you think of my poster?'

He unrolled this glossy paper thing. You could tell he thought it was wonderful. *Cabaret for Barcelona* it said in big neat letters. And all around the edge were pictures of flamenco dancers and guitars and bulls and matadors and shiny hot suns. They'd all been chosen from some clip-art file. Of course.

Mr Originality.

I wanted to say, 'You can put your chips in it.'

TONSILLITIS

Sometimes, I get tonsillitis, which is terrific fun I don't think. I get this lumpy feeling in my throat and then I know it's started. Before long it's *so* grot, all I can do is sip a drink.

When it happens, I lie on the sofa with a hot water-bottle and watch the television. Princess Pathetic.

I suppose I've seen a lot of tonsil telly but I like the old films the best. Especially the black and white ones. They say things like *I know darling, it's all so terribly beastly.* Of course, fifty years ago the old films were the new films, weren't they? And people actually queued to see them. Now they show them on daytime TV, for people with sore throats. Like me.

On Tuesday, I'd woken up feeling double yuck.

'Mum,' I croaked.

Mum knew the routine. By the time she went to work I was *really* out of it. And I wasn't much better on Wednesday. But I watched this film about Admiral Nelson and that helped a lot. He's the one on top of the column — the one covered in pigeon poo. Well, pigeons don't care, do they?

Dad came home early to see how I was.

'How's your throat, Smidge?' he asked.

'Sore,' I whispered. When you have tonsillitis, you keep your answers short.

'Need anything? Honey and lemon?'

'Please.'

When Dad came back with the drink, I tried to make an effort. It was thinking about Admiral Nelson that did it. A sore throat wouldn't have bothered him. No way. He'd probably have started a jolly sea shanty or something. I mean, he lost an eye and he lost an arm and he still got on with it. You had to in those days.

'Here you are, Smidge.'

'Thanks, Dad.'

'D'you want the good news or the bad news?' he asked.

'Um . . .' I didn't really know.

'Well the good news is we've been invited to Choir of Choirs!'

'That's brilliant, Dad!' Ouch! That hurt.

And it really *was* brilliant. Because if you're a Welsh choir then Choir of Choirs is about as good as it gets. It happens every year at the Royal Albert Hall. Loads of choirs get together for a massive concert. Imagine that – half the world's blazers in one building! So it's really big time to get asked to sing. Mr Williams was always going on about it. I bet he'd buy himself a new conducting stick.

   'Apparently,' explained Dad, 'Aberdare Male Voice has dropped out so there's a chance for us. Mr Williams phoned me at work. It's short notice mind, but Choir of Choirs is . . .'
   'Special,' I said.

'Exactly!' Dad paused for a moment. 'But the thing is, Smidge, it's the same day as the Cabaret for Barcelona.'

Which meant they couldn't sing at my school! I felt like punching the air. It was the best bad news ever.

'Never mind,' I said, dead sincere.

'I feel as if we're letting you down.'

'Oh no!' I tried not to look too happy.

'Karen's mum says not to worry. She's got some other ideas. So the cabaret will go on just the same.'

'Great.' My throat began to feel OK.

'Yes,' said Dad. 'Apparently Eddie's dad's going to sing some Elvis songs.'

EDDIE'S BIG WORRY

I felt a lot better on Thursday. I even got properly dressed. Not first thing of course, but eventually. I wanted to get on with my poster.

I propped up my Gaudi book against a big pot and put my rough design right next to it. Then I opened up my best art pad and got to work. I filled the paper with a pencil drawing of The Sacred Family and spent ages trying to get everything just right. But it looked all wrong. So I scrunched it up and threw it away. Like I did the next one. And the next! But I wasn't giving up, no way, and my fourth drawing was much better. I did it more quickly and didn't worry about the details so much. It

was more of an impression. Then I drew BARCELONA in great big letters across the top. I made them look like they were floating in the sky behind the church. And curved round – like an imaginary horizon. I was dead careful to get the spacings just right and kept checking with my rough design. I didn't want to get to BARCELO and run out of paper, did I?

Well, when I stood back and checked what I'd done, I knew I'd got it right. Sometimes you just do.

'Unscrunchable!' I said out loud.

But I decided to finish it off in Art class. I wanted to show Miss Dapple and see what she thought. I knew she'd like it.

I'd started to tidy things up when someone knocked on the door.

It was Eddie, wasn't it? He'd come round straight from school. He asked me how I was – blah blah blah – then he got to the point.

'Have you heard what's happened?' He looked dead miserable. I could guess why. 'My dad's singing at the cabaret.'

'I know,' I said.

'How?'

'Well, my dad told me.'

'You see,' he groaned. 'Your dad knows. You know. Soon the whole world's going to know! It's going to be just awful!'

I'd like to have disagreed with him, but I couldn't. 'Does Malcolm Marmalade know?' I asked.

'Not yet. But he's going to, isn't he?

Karen told everyone that her mum's found an Elvis singer. Malcolm thought that was totally hilarious.' Eddie put his head in his hands.

'So Karen didn't say it was your dad?'

'Not yet. But she's going to find out, isn't she? And then she'll tell everyone.'

'Not if we get to her first,' I said.

The trick is to say these things like you mean them.

WE GET TO KAREN

I went back to school on Friday. I could have stayed off 'til Monday but I wanted to get to Karen.

We cornered her inside the gates. Me and Sally.

'Karen,' I said. 'Can we have a word?'

'Sure,' said Karen, looking a bit puzzled.

'I hear your mum's found an Elvis singer,' I said.

'I know! Isn't it brilliant! He's some new parent, apparently.' You could tell Karen thought we'd explode into giggles or something. But we didn't.

'He's Eddie's dad,' I said straight out.

Karen's mouth opened a little. 'Really?'

'Really,' I said.

'And if anyone starts making fun,' Sally explained, 'it's going to be so unfair.'

'That's right,' I agreed. 'I mean, after all, it's your mum who wants him to sing.'

'And it's not like Eddie's going to Barcelona,' Sally pointed out.

'And you just *know* how Malcolm will go on and on.'

'OK,' said Karen, like it was all a fuss about nothing. 'I won't mention it, and if I'm asked who Elvis is, I'll say he's someone's dad in Year Ten.'

'Right.'

'Right.'

'And . . . thanks.'

'No probs.'

Karen's all right.

She was Eddie's new confidante.

And the three of us went off to find him.

FINISHING THE POSTER

I was right about Miss Dapple. She did like my poster.

'You could use a colour wash for the building,' she said. 'Then it would look like you painted it from life but were only there a few minutes.'

'OK.' I thought that was a brilliant idea. 'But what about all the lettering?'

'Well, Sam, with a poster the important thing is to grab people's attention. Once you've done that, you're halfway there. Of course, some people go through life with their eyes closed. But forget about them and think about the others. Ask yourself – who is it you want to read the poster and what's most important to them? How can you grab their attention?'

Miss Dapple always makes you think. She makes you see that some-times simple things are complicated and complicated things are simple. But she never tells you what to do. She only makes suggestions or asks questions.

So I did quite a bit of thinking before I knew how to finish my poster. But it wasn't that hard. I'm quite good at making my mind up.

I rubbed out the letters in the sky, even though they looked dead good – because I needed the space for something different. I needed to get the point of the poster across. So I drew *Cabaret for Barcelona* instead.

Mooningbum would probably say I was copying him. But I wasn't. No way. It just happened to be the right words. Even duff-buckets can get things right sometimes. I also used big letters for the date – *Fri 14 March*. I drew that at the bottom on the left and I wrote all the other stuff on the right. It didn't matter that the words were small because, if nobody wanted to read them, I wouldn't have grabbed their attention, would I?

That was all the drawing done.

So I mixed up my colour wash, which was a sort of sandy brown, and I sploshed it on with a big fat brush. It was fun being messy. Finally, I painted in the bigger letters as carefully as I could. I chose deep-blue and plum-purple for that because they're the colours of Barcelona Football Club. Eddie told me that. He was sitting in the next chair.

And saying all the right things . . .

'That's a great poster, Sam.'

'Thanks, Eddie,' I said looking down at his. I won't describe it. You wouldn't be impressed.

'What d'you think of mine?' he asked.

'Well . . .' I tried to find the right word.

'It's rubbish, isn't it?' he suggested.

Rubbish was a good word.

'Well . . .' I hesitated.

'Useless?'

Useless would have done just as well.

'Well . . .'

I was about to say it was *interesting* – Princess Diplomat – but, lucky for me, Eddie changed the subject.

'I keep thinking about my dad,' he said. 'I can't think about anything else.'

'But we've sorted that.' I said the words but I knew we hadn't. We'd only slowed things down. And Eddie knew it.

'He's still going to sing,' he said, 'and he'll tell everyone he's my dad. I know what he's like. Even if I ask him not to. He thinks everything's just a big laugh. He doesn't realize what Malcolm Middleton will do when he finds out.'

And Mooningbum was going to find out. Sooner or later. But what could we do?

'Maybe your dad'll catch tonsillitis and lose his voice?' I said as a joke. I hoped it might cheer Eddie up, but it didn't. He just sort of grunted. So I had another go. 'Well maybe he'll get a better offer. You know, like my dad did with their choir thing. Maybe he'll get Elvis of Elvises.'

Eddie looked at me like a dog in a pet shop.

A CHANGE OF DATE AND A CHANGE OF PLAN

With less than three weeks to go we finally got the posters up. We stuck them all around the school entrance and in the corridors. Everybody said mine was the biz – apart from Malcolm, of course. But I could tell he was jealous. Anyone could see his poster was one big yawn. But Sally's wasn't. She'd drawn a spotlight falling on a microphone. It looked like a nightclub or something and it grabbed your attention. But mine was the best. I'm not bragging – it just was!

Eddie managed not to finish his poster. Eddie's no fool.

But we got our posters up.

And then they changed the date!

Brilliant or what?

Apparently half the teachers had been landed with some meeting that clashed. Karen said her mum spent all evening on the phone. I know she called Mr Williams because he called our house.

'D'you want the good news or the good news?' Dad asked, hanging up the phone.

'How about the good news?' I said. I had my suspicions – in fact, my fingers were crossed so hard they hurt.

It didn't work.

'We're singing at your school after all!' Dad announced with a big grin.

'Great,' I said.

I think he believed me. Maybe I should be an actress.

In case you're wondering, we changed our posters by sticking the new date – March 21 – over the old one. It wasn't a massive deal – it didn't get reported on the six o'clock news or anything.

20

A TERRIBLE DAY OUT

My mum says some days you should stay in bed. I know just what she means. And I bet Eddie does too. He should definitely have pulled up the duvet the day we went to Cadbury World.

When I got to school I was feeling all right. What with no classes and the thought of free chocolate, who wouldn't be? The sun was even shining and I expect the birds were singing. But I can't swear to that. Anyway, the point is, I was ready to forget about Welsh choirs and Elvis singers and get on with an OK day away.

Then I walked through the school gates. And there he was – right in my face – spouting off to Julie and Jack.

Malcolm Muckspreader.

'We had the plumber yesterday for our new jacuzzi.' He gave me this big smirky look. 'And it was Eddie's dad. He told my mum all about the cabaret.'

Oh no! I thought.

'Oh good,' I said. Show no fear.

'And what did he tell her?' Julie was lapping it up, wasn't she?

'Eddie's dad is going to be Elvis Presley.' Mildew looked triumphant. 'With an Elvis wig and stupid clothes. He does it all the time, my mum says. Imagine having a dad who thinks he's Elvis Presley! My dad can't wait to see him.'

Julie and Jack creased up.

'He doesn't think he's

Elvis,' I said. 'It's an impersonation. He does it for charity. And for a laugh.'

'Well we're all laughing!' Muckspreader spluttered. 'So why aren't you? Is it because your dad's Welshy choir are going to be up there with him? Maybe they could sing together?'

That was just hilarious, I can tell you.

'When I get to Barcelona and you're stuck here, we'll see who's laughing then!' It was the best I could do, I'm afraid.

'Ooooh!' said Julie holding up her invisible handbag.

Julie was dead!

'Oh look! Here comes Eddie.' Moronicus was really enjoying himself.

'That's it. I'm off,' I said. I needed to get to Eddie.

But Eddie had guessed already. He'd seen it in their faces and the way they'd looked across, laughing.

Well, after that, our trip to Cadbury

World was a total nightmare. On the coach, me and Eddie sat near Mr Worthington. Can you imagine? In fact we stuck by him the whole day practically. That way Mustypants couldn't get to Eddie – except of course with his nasty smirky looks.

One day, when I get the chance, I'll have to go back to Cadbury World, because it looked like a lot of fun. But that day, dragging round with Mr W, keeping away from Mooningbum, I couldn't enjoy any of it.

Not properly. Not even the free chocolate! All I did was get through it. It was a rotten day.

Mooningbum wasn't even sick!

And I don't know why I felt *so* responsible for Eddie. But I did. I even walked home with him after.

'I could kill my dad,' he moaned. 'I told him not to mention his Elvis singing. But he never listens. And then he thinks everyone will see the joke. He thinks they're laughing *with* him. He doesn't see that they're laughing *at* him.'

'I know what you mean!' I said – as if my dad was just the same.

But he wasn't the same. My dad wasn't Mr Cool, I knew that. And I wouldn't be mouthing off about his choir coming to the school. No way! But I wasn't *that* embarrassed, not deep down, not like Eddie was.

'If only he could see himself,' said Eddie.

EDDIE HAS A SICKIE

When Eddie didn't come to school the next day, I decided I'd check him out. I suppose he might have gone down with something dead catching, but somehow I felt he hadn't.

And I was right.

'I couldn't face school,' he explained. 'Not after yesterday. So I told my mum I felt sick and had a headache.'

'I don't blame you,' I said, meaning it.

'Was anything said? About my dad and everything. Did Malcolm make a load of jokes?'

'Not really,' I lied. 'He said a few stupid things – but then he always does. No one laughed. Not much anyway.'

The truth was that Moron had really given Eddie the treatment. Big time. And all the drongos had just loved joining in. Me and Sally and Karen had done what we could to shut them up, but it wasn't easy. Robbie Jones had come up to me all giggly and asked if I thought Eddie's dad would split his tight trousers? Oh ha ha! I could have said something dead cutting about his mum, but I didn't. I played it cool instead.

And that's how it was all day. But why tell Eddie? He was suffering enough already.

'Are you coming back tomorrow?' I asked.

'I think I'll have to.'

'I'll meet you at the gates.'

'Thanks.'

When I had the earache I saw this film called *Butch Cassidy and the Sundance Kid*. In the final scene, the two heroes rush out from their hidey shelter and there's a whole army waiting to shoot them down.

That's just how it would feel at the school gates.

GETTING THROUGH IT

Well, we got Eddie through that Friday. Just about. It wasn't easy. But we got him through it. Of course, Mustypants had a wonderful time stirring it, didn't he? And all the drongos acted like he was king of comedy. But me and Eddie and Sally and Karen just kept ignoring them. And, in the end, it seemed to work. In fact, by going-home time, Moron's pathetic jokes were obviously wearing thin. Julie was still doing her nasty stupid smile, but even she'd stopped laughing.

And then we got a two-day break.

So, when Monday came round, I didn't feel like Butch Cassidy any more. My dad's choir were going to sing and so was Eddie's dad. Well, so what! And anyway, it would get me and Sally to Barcelona, wouldn't it?

I mean, I had a life.

Then along came Choir of Choirs.

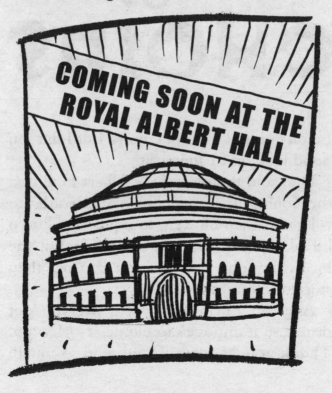

23

CHOIR OF CHOIRS

I didn't go to Choir of Choirs. But I did say good luck and I meant it.

Dad said they loved the Albert Hall and the sound was incredible. Afterwards, to celebrate, they all went to a pub and had a bit of a party. You can imagine what the locals thought. I mean, you can bet they started singing in Welsh.

Anyway, during the party Mervyn got drunk, so if anyone's to blame, it's Mervyn. Thank you, Mervyn. Thank you so much!

They were talking about the cabaret and he said it would be *fabulous* to dress like Elvis. Not stupid or tragic or gross but *fabulous*. And – get this – two of the choir agreed with him! Can you believe it? Two of them? Don't ask me who they were. And don't ask me why they agreed. Maybe they were fed up with the purple blazers. Maybe they thought it would be hilarious. I didn't know and I didn't really care. The point was, two of them agreed!

Now if I told you Mr Williams loved the idea, you'd call me a liar, wouldn't you?

So go on, call me a liar!

You're dead right. Mr Williams hated the idea.

BUT . . .

. . . he gave them a lecture on the *purity of tradition*! Can you believe it? They'd just done this big concert and were having this drink up – and he gives them a stupid lecture! My dad did a brilliant impression when he told me. I could just see Mr Williams standing there.

'*Now boys, the male voice choir has a rich and proud history . . .*'

I wish I'd been there, I'd have told them straight. 'Never mind all that rubbish, what about my life?'

But I wasn't there, was I? And he was. And he must've really got up their noses because it started this massive row, apparently. And in the end, seven of the choir, including my dad, said perhaps it would be fun. Perhaps they should dress as Elvis and sing along with Eddie's dad!

SEVEN!

INCLUDING my dad!

What was he thinking?

Of course, the next morning, it wasn't such a brilliantly hilarious idea. Like it ever had been! And it didn't do to upset Mr Williams, did it? Dad was on the telephone half the morning.

BUT ... Mr Williams had this huge sulk on!

He said that the choir would have to decide where it stood. He said he wouldn't conduct another beat until it was sorted. He said he wouldn't be at the Sunday rehearsal. He said lots of other stuff too, but I expect you get the idea.

My mum got it right. 'Well I hope you can talk some sense into them,' she said to my dad.

'I'll try,' he said, 'but I feel like I'm stuck in the middle. I mean there are two sides to every argument.'

'Dad!' I said. 'You'll be singing at *my* school. And anyway, what will Eddie's dad think?'

'Yes I know that, but there are two sides,' he repeated.

'Right!' I said. 'There's Mr Williams' side and there's the totally stupid moronic side!'

Imagine that – me sticking up for Mr Williams and the purity of the tradition!

'OK, Smidge. I get the point.'

And I thought he had. I really did. I thought he'd go in there and sort them out. Even Mervyn.

So when Sunday night came and he

went off to choir praccy, I was feeling OK. Just about. I mean, I was breathing in and breathing out. Chocolate tasted like chocolate. My life still had meaning. Or so I thought!

I was still up when Dad got back.

'Well?' I asked.

'Well, Smidge,' he said. 'It's a bit awkward.'

'What d'you mean?' I had this terrible feeling I wasn't going to like it.

And I was dead right.

Because – get this – Dad said Mervyn wouldn't back down. He argued that the power would go to Mr Williams' head. There was this huge discussion, apparently, and at the end of it Mervyn had most people agreeing. Can you believe it!

And so . . .

As long as Eddie's dad was OK with the idea, and as long as they can get the costumes, twelve of them agreed to do it. And *my dad* was one of them! After all I'd said to him!

Aaaaaaaagh!

It was going to be some sort of protest –

something dead significant but fun. Oh yeah! The point they were all missing was they wanted to dress like Elvis Presley and sing AT MY SCHOOL.

It would just be a one-off, my dad said. And after, they'd go back to Mr Williams and his blazers. But so what?

By then, my life would be over.

MALCOLM LEARNS THE NEWS

I caught Eddie at the school gates. And I didn't like his expression. It sort of told me what I didn't want to know.

'Eddie,' I said, hoping I was wrong.

'You're going to ask about the Elvis Choir, aren't you?'

'Oh no!' I groaned.

'My dad got the call last night,' he said. 'Someone called Mervyn rang. Of course my dad thinks it's a great idea. They were on the phone for ages.'

I think I kind of whimpered.

* * *

Word got round double quick, didn't it? But then I knew it would. I mean, it wasn't the sort of thing you kept quiet about – thirteen Elvis singers all on one stage! Robbie Jones seemed to know first thing on Tuesday. It was him who told Mustardbreath.

Of course, Malcolm thought it was the best news ever – and obviously the *only* thing worth talking about.

'I didn't know Elvis was Welsh!' Ha ha.

'My dad's going to take photos!' Ho ho.

'They could start a football team!' Hee hee.

I won't tell you the dead clever answers I used to put him down, because there weren't any. I just spent the whole day soaking it up. But I never burst into angry tears – though I did come close when I ran into Sally's mum.

'Is everything all right, Sam?' she asked. 'You look a bit upset.'

'It's OK, Mum,' said Sally.

And I'm glad she was there, because if I'd had to speak I think I might have lost it. Then Malcolm and the drongos would have won.

It was a rotten day. I never want to live through another one like it.

And you know what? Eddie was just amazing. I mean, it was just as bad for him and he'd already had it double bad. But somehow he kind of got through it better than me.

I had a right go at my dad that night.

'I'm sorry, Smidge,' he said after I'd calmed down a bit. 'I'm sorry you're getting a hard time at school.'

'But I told you how it would be!'

'Yes, but it's what the rest of the choir wants and I have to go along with them or there'll just be another big row. Besides, it's just a bit of fun and you always say we take ourselves too seriously.'

'And are you actually going to sing *all* Elvis songs?'

'Well, providing we can rehearse them up in time. At least, that's our plan.'

'But . . .'

'But what?'

'But nothing.' I was stuck with it, wasn't I?

I was just off to bed when Eddie rang.

'Sam . . .' he said after a bit of a pause.

'Yes?' I wondered what was coming next.

'I'm going to see the cabaret.'

'You're what?' I hadn't expected that, I can tell you.

'I had a long talk with my dad and he

says, if it really bothers me he'll stop being Elvis. But I have to see him at school. I have to see him one more time.'

'But why?' I asked.

'He says it's funny and I'm missing the point.'

'*You're* missing the point!'

'I know. But I've said I'll go. Then maybe he'll stop.'

'Right. Well, that's good isn't it?'

'The thing is . . .'

'Yes?' I wondered what the thing was.

'Will you come with me?'

What could I say?

ELVISWEAR

You won't believe how easy it is to hire Elviswear.

I'd hoped it wouldn't be. I'd hoped the whole stupid scheme would fall apart without wigs and things. And I'd hoped wigs were hard to find.

But they're not. Nor are the other things. Not even jumpsuits.

How scary is that?

Of course Eddie's dad knew just where to look. Thanks very much! Dad said his help was *invaluable* — which isn't the word

I'd have used. I mean, you'd think he'd have had something better to do, wouldn't you? Like plumbing perhaps. You'd think some big hotel would need its bathrooms sorting. But no.

When my dad tried on his outfit, my mum doubled up. She was like something from a silent movie. You could see she was laughing but you couldn't hear her. When

something's really funny, she stops breathing. Don't ask me why.

'What d'you think?' asked Dad.

Mum still couldn't speak.

I could, but I didn't. I thought instead about dropping to the floor and sobbing. I thought about gnashing my teeth – if *gnashing* is what I think it is. I thought about a lot of stuff actually. But before I could do any of it, someone rang the doorbell.

'I'll go,' said Dad.

I practically knocked him down getting there first.

It was only Sally. Thank goodness.

When *she* stopped laughing, she told me, 'My mum says I can go along tomorrow if I keep right out of the way and maybe wash a few glasses.'

'What!' I said. 'You mean you want to come too?'

'Of course.'

26

THE
CABARET

We didn't wash any glasses, but we kept out of the way. You bet we did! If they'd drilled a hole in the wall, I'd have stood behind it. Then I'd have plugged it up with chewing gum and stuck my head in a bucket. That's how much I wanted to be there.

The school hall felt different somehow. The big windows were blacked out with sheets of paper and the lights were all turned off. But there were candles on the tables we use for lunch and the stage was lit up with the red and blue lamps from the drama studio.

Around the tables, drinking wine and eating nuts, were all the parents and teachers.

The room was really full.

Why is there never a fire when you need one? Just a small one would have done.

'Who's that right at the front?' said Eddie. 'Isn't that Malcolm's mum and dad?'

Eddie was dead right. Sitting bang in the middle were Mr Sunday Golf and Mrs Jacuzzi.

'They'll tell Malcolm everything,' added Sally. Thanks. Like we needed reminding!

At ten to nine, Karen's mum got up on the stage.

'I think it's about to start,' said Eddie.

And it was.

Karen's mum bent into the microphone. Why are microphones never at the right height?

Well thank you, ladies and gentlemen,' she said, 'and welcome to our Cabaret for Barcelona.'

Karen was lucky not to be there, I can

tell you. Her mum was dead nervous and went on and on for ages telling everybody what they knew already.

'We hope to raise a lot of money tonight.'

Like they'd be there for some other reason!

'So let's all sit back and enjoy the show.'

I thought, *In your dreams!*

'And here to get things underway is a piece of classic modern comedy. So let's give a big warm welcome to Rosie Jones.'

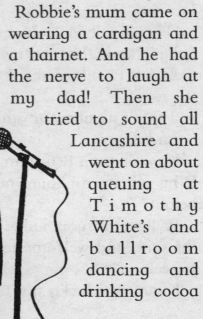

Robbie's mum came on wearing a cardigan and a hairnet. And he had the nerve to laugh at my dad! Then she tried to sound all Lancashire and went on about queuing at Timothy White's and ballroom dancing and drinking cocoa and wearing slippers at the bus stop and varicose veins and stuff. And, get this, for some strange reason, people found it funny. Don't ask me why! It must have been the wine or something. But maybe I missed the point. I mean, I wasn't exactly in a hilarious mood.

'Well that was wonderful,' said Karen's mum when the applause died down. 'And now for our next act, and as a special surprise, please welcome our very own Jim Worthington and Billy.'

'Our very own who?' I muttered.

Well, old Elbow Patches walked on stage with this ancient ventriloquist dummy dressed like a sailor. It looked like he'd rescued it from the *Titanic*.

'He's never going to make it talk,' whispered Sally.

And he didn't. But what he did do was make the thing mime along to this old song that started coming out the speakers.

I think it's called *Bohemian Rhapsody*. And I suppose you could just about imagine the dummy was singing. If you really tried. I'm afraid I didn't much, but I was impressed that Mr W had the bottle.

'Imagine Mr Worthington doing ventriloquism,' said Sally when he'd finished his bit.

'Karaoke ventriloquism,' I pointed out. I suppose it was quite original if you thought about it. And he did get a nice round of applause.

'Well, that was wonderful,' said Karen's mum with a big smile. 'And right now, we'll take a very short break. But don't go away!'

Don't go away! I wish I'd had the chance.

'I feel a bit sick,' said Eddie. I knew how he felt. I mean, we could see what was coming next.

At the side of the stage the choir was getting ready.

'Let's go and wish them good luck,' suggested Sally.

Eddie and I gave her exactly the same look.

'OK,' she said. 'Let's not!'

And anyway, there wasn't time. Because Karen's mum was moving back to the microphone. She'd said the break would be short. Another two weeks would have suited me.

'This is it then,' Eddie gulped.

I screwed up my eyes and tried to imagine it wasn't happening. But it was.

'And now ladies and gentlemen, for the very first time, and for one performance

only . . . please welcome the one and only
Elvis Presley Male Voice Choir.'

Help!

On they came. All thirteen of them. The
laughter started straight away.

My life was definitely over.

They stood in a line just like they would
for Mr Williams. And with the same blank

expressions behind their huge naff sunglasses. Dad was near the middle. I thought, *Maybe they won't recognize him.* But I knew they would. The costumes were all different but similar – if you know what I mean – awful white jumpsuits and ghastly black wigs. Two of the choir had ugly fat bellies. Like they didn't look stupid enough!

Mervyn was the most glam. He definitely had the most glitter. He made my dad look almost dull. Which was quite an achievement, believe me.

Eddie's dad stood at the end with his guitar.

When the laughter died a bit, he strummed a chord and stepped up to the microphone.

Don't ask me, but straight off I knew the song – *Blue Suede Shoes*.

Eddie put his head in his hands.

My mouth went all dry. The choir didn't move a muscle. Not even a twitch. They just let Eddie's dad Elvis his way through the song.

Until he got to the chorus. And then they started.

But they sang the way they did for Mr Williams – like they were dead from the neck down.

They even did harmonies.

And at the end of the song – the school

hall went crazy! I could hardly believe it. Everybody cheered and stamped and clapped and whistled. I didn't know the School Association had it in them.

I looked at Eddie and he looked at me. Puzzled is how we looked. But Sally was smiling and clapping her hands.

'Great,' she said, not joking.

The next song started before the hall quietened down. It was a slow one called *Love Me Tender.*

Eddie's dad stood with the choir and, this time, they all sang together. In my head, I could see Mr Williams standing out front waving his arms.

'This is brilliant,' said Sally beaming.

'Is it?' said Eddie.

'D'you think so?' I added.

'Of course. Look at everyone!'

So we did.

And everyone was smiling. Not sneering or smirking. But smiling. Then – at the end of the song – cheering and clapping. Again!

I still couldn't believe it.

But that's how it went. Song after song.

Don't ask me how they learned them – *Heartbreak Hotel, It's Now or Never, Hound Dog, All Shook Up, Return to Sender, Are You Lonesome Tonight*?

In the fast songs people were laughing out loud. It was the way the choir looked. And the way they sounded. It was all wrong and all right – but at the same time! And Eddie's dad was amazing as the front man. Sort of funny serious. People had tears in their eyes. Mum was doing her silent movie laugh.

And in the slow songs, everybody smiled along. Mr Williams should have been there. It was his own stupid fault he wasn't!

Their very last song was *Jailhouse Rock*, and for this one they did a little dance! They must have saved it up. It looked like rock and roll for people with arthritis and blue suede shoes a size too small.

It was totally awesome. Funnier than anything on the television. Easily! And people were laughing WITH them.

And – get this – a few of the parents got up and started *dancing* along! I think it's called the jive or something. And the best thing was two of the dancers were Mr Sunday Golf and Mrs Jacuzzi! Well, the way he threw himself about was a total hoot. I mean, you couldn't *not* look at him and laugh. I bet he suffered the next morning!

It was just brilliant!

And when it was over, when people finally stopped cheering and stuff – which took ages – Eddie and I did high fives.

'Yes!' I said.

'Wicked!'

'They're all stars,' said Sally.

Sally was dead right.

'We never doubted it, did we Eddie?'

'Never!'

BACK AT SCHOOL

We got to the wall early that Monday. Me and Eddie and Sally and Karen. We wanted to be there when Malcolm arrived. Because this time we were ready for him. You bet we were!

If he said one stupid word, we'd let him have it. And Julie too – if she started.

In my head, I'd written a script.

Oh, how interesting you still think it's such a big joke! Because everybody said it was the best thing they've seen for years. Sally's mum said she'll still be laughing at the memory when we all get to Barcelona. And we'll still be laughing too, especially when we think about your dad and his wild dancing.

Of course he didn't show, did he? But he was at school – he sneaked in round the back. Mr Bravery! And he kept away from us all day. Don't ask me where he ate his lunch. Probably he went home for chips.

But we had a brilliant day – even if we didn't get to Mustyface. Miss Dapple said Elvis Presley would never sound the same again. And she's a big fan apparently, which surprised me a bit. Then we talked loads about Gaudi and buildings and what a brilliant time I'd have in Spain. And it was great to see Eddie laughing about his dad the way he did – like he was out there on top of things.

And best of all – at going-home time, Jack's mum was outside.

'Sam,' she called. 'Can I have a word?'

I went across. 'Hello.'

'I did so enjoy your father's choir,' she said. 'And so did my friend.'

'Oh good.' I wondered who her friend was.

'He's an old chum from my TV days. He happened to be here for the weekend. I didn't introduce him on Saturday because he had to get away. But . . .'

'Yes?'

'He rang me today. He thinks the Elvis Presley Male Voice Choir should go to the Edinburgh Festival and he wants to set it up!'

28

AND . . .

So.

Just to remind you.

Jack's mum was in *Grange Hill*.

Karen's dad played football for Notts Forest.

Julie's uncle's got a Rolls Royce. So she says.

Bipin's dad sailed round the world.

Sally's mum speaks five languages. And one of them's Russian!

But my dad sings in the Elvis Presley Choir.

And so does Eddie's.

THE WAR DIARIES OF ALISTAIR FURY

BUGS ON THE BRAIN
Jamie Rix

BONSAI!
THIS IS
WAR

My big brother and sister, William and Mel, may be older
than me and biggerer than me, but they're not cleverer than
me. Just because the chips of the world are stacked against
me like a potato mountain doesn't mean they can beat me.
Revenge will be mine!

Or rather mine and the Revengers', and a boa constrictor
called Alfred's. Let loose the snakes of doom and see how
they like it then! I shall have my revenge before you can say
'peanut butter and jam sandwiches'! Actually I shouldn't
have mentioned peanut butter and jam sandwiches. Forget
you ever read that. If you don't, I may have to kill you.

The first book in a brilliant and hilarious series by
award-winning comic writer, Jamie Rix.

CORGI YEARLING BOOKS
ISBN 0440 864763

RESCUING DAD
Pete Johnson

'How do you improve your dad?'

Joe and Claire can see why Mum chucked Dad out. He
looks a mess, he can't cook and he's useless around the
house. Something must be done: they're the only ones who
can help transform him into 'Dad Mark Two'. And when
they unveil this new, improved dad, Mum will be so
impressed she'll take him back on the spot!

But then disaster strikes – Mum starts seeing the slimy
and creepy Roger. And Joe and Claire's plans take an
unexpected turn – with hilarious results.

'Pete Johnson is a wonderful story-teller' *Evening Standard*

'An author of exceptional talents…sensitive, humorous and
down-to-earth' *School Librarian*

CORGI YEARLING BOOKS
ISBN 0440 864577